The Heavy Bag
One Girl's Journey Through Grief

By Sarah Surgey
Illustrated by Larisa Ivankovic

The Heavy Bag

AUTHOR: Sarah Surgey

ILLUSTRATOR: Larisa Ivankovic

RELEASE DATE: April 1, 2024
32 pages • 8.25 x 10.25 • Ages 4 to 10

ISBN (HARDCOVER):
978-1-945369-4-1-4 • $17.95 USD

ISBN (EBOOK):
978-1-945369-5-1-3 • $4.99 USD

LEXILE LEVELING: 490L

GUIDED READING: M

THEMES: Grief • loss • feelings • emotions PSHE learning • SEL

UNIQUE FEATURES

- This book has been translated into 14 languages
- Tips and questions for parents and caregivers to ask before, during and after reading
- Beyond the book section with resources on 5 stages of grief and activity
- FREE Reader's Guide and coloring pages available at www.cardinalrulepress.com

MARKETING EFFORTS

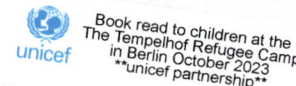
Book read to children at the The Tempelhof Refugee Camp in Berlin October 2023
unicef partnership

- National media & promotion
- Influencer outreach campaign (1K average account reach)
- Navigating Grief with Children (March 2024) feature
- Book trailer on YouTube (3K channel subscribers, average 13K views)
- Advertising in Edelweiss
- Email Marketing (21K list)
- Author blog tour
- Educator, librarian & bookseller outreach
- Digital assets available (Reader's Guide, Coloring pages)
- Author appearances
- Goodreads giveaway (2000+ participants)
- Facebook giveaway (750+ new leads)
- LibraryThing Giveaway (400+ participants)

COMPARISON BOOKS:

- **The Hare Shaped Hole**
  (Frances Lincoln Children's Books, 2023)
  ISBN: 978-0711276055

- **Lost in the Clouds**
  (DK Books, 2021) ISBN: 978-0241488034

- **When Sadness Comes to Call**
  (Andersen Press, 2020)
  ISBN: 978-1783447954

SOME OF OUR AWARD WINNING TITLES

MORE THAN 4 MILLION BOOKS SOLD!

 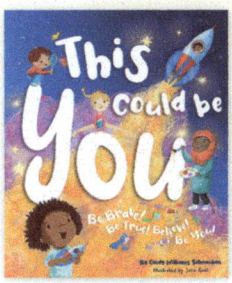 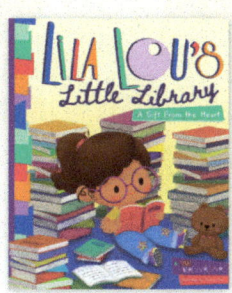 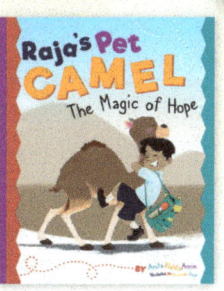
  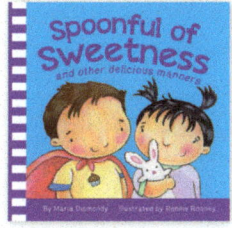 
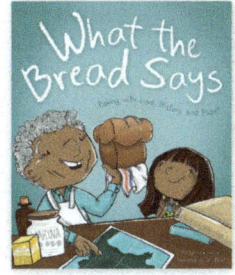 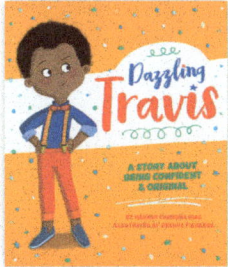 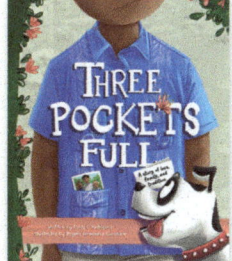 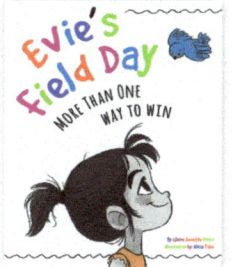
 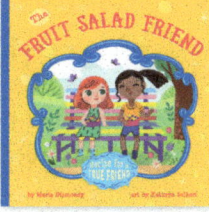  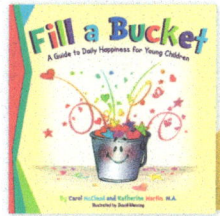

CHECK OUT OUR CATALOG

SCAN HERE

KIDS' INDIE NEXT LIST
Please consider this book!

SUBMISSION DEADLINE IS JANUARY 8, 2024

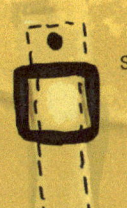 

Enid had feelings, feelings she had never felt before. The feelings arrived the day her grandpa died.

After he died, Enid put all the special things they had shared in her bag and set off on the path they used to walk together.

She knew it would be easier to walk without all the special things in her bag, but she couldn't just leave them at home. She wanted to keep them safe and close.

With each step, her bag grew heavier and a great big mix of feelings whooshed down from her head to her toes,

making her feel dizzy.

And **heavy**.

She stomped ahead until...

"Wow," the girl behind the stand said, "that's a really big bag! What do you have in there?"

"None of your business!" said Enid.

"You sound angry," Margo said.

Enid could feel her cheeks start to burn and her legs wobble. She wanted to scream. Instead, she took off the heavy bag, and pulled out a cracked telescope.

"Grandpa said he would look at the stars with me," she said, "but now he's gone."

"You're carrying so much; it's hard for you to walk,"
Margo said softly.

"I'm happy you decided to talk.

Let me hold this for you and lighten your load.

You are not alone as you walk this road."

Passing over the telescope, Enid pictured a smile beneath Grandpa's fluffy gray mustache.

When she put her bag back on, it felt lighter.

Back on the path, Enid drew a line as she walked. When she came to a stream, she felt so sad that she had to stop and rest.

"What's the matter, dear?" asked a neighbor walking his dog.

"I lost my grandpa," she said.

"I'm sorry," he said. "That looks like a heavy bag. What is inside?"

"A wooden boat that Grandpa made with me. We were going to sail it together," Enid said with a cry.

"Let it out," the man said. "You're carrying so much; it's hard for you to walk. I'm happy you decided to talk. Let me hold this for you and lighten your load. You are not alone as you walk this road."

Enid handed the boat to her neighbor and watched as he took it to the water.

"We can watch it sail off on its journey together," he smiled.

Enid said goodbye and picked up the bag.

It didn't hurt her shoulders anymore.

But soon the dizzy feelings whooshed

through her body again,

and "what ifs" circled her mind.

What if she had visited Grandpa that morning? Would his heart not have broken?

What if she had told him she was baking for him?

Would he have waited for her?

What if...

"Whoa!"

"Well, hello there!" said Ida, a lady Enid knew.

"Why do you look so sad?"

"I lost my grandpa."

Enid felt tears in her eyes again.

"I made some biscuits for him.
I won't be able to give
them to him."

"You're carrying so much; it's hard for you to walk," the lady said.
"I'm happy you decided to talk. Let me hold this for you
and lighten your load. You are not alone as you walk this road.
I know some birds that would love some biscuits."

Enid reached inside her bag and handed it to Ida.

They smiled at each other.

Enid felt different now.

She felt light as a feather.

The sun had found its way through the clouds

and she spotted a rainbow.

Before long, Enid arrived at the end of her street.

She looked across the road at Grandpa's house.

The bag was much lighter.

She had let friends help her carry the heavy things.

What remained were the special things:

MEMORIES

And the memories weighed... nothing at all! They were light and lovely. She could carry them wherever she went.

Did You Know there are 5 STAGES OF GRIEF?

DENIAL: This is our brain's way of tricking us into thinking that sad things haven't really happened. It helps us to not feel so overwhelmed in the early days of an event.

ANGER: Although anger can seem upsetting to others, it's actually how you begin healing. This is an essential emotion and will eventually fade. Try telling someone you trust how anger feels and why you feel angry.

BARGAINING: As your anger fades, it makes way for 'bargaining.' You might feel that if you had done/not done something differently, your loved one wouldn't have died. This is untrue, but it's natural to feel/think this way.

DEPRESSION: Another word for this is 'sadness.' Of course, you feel sad and that's OK. Remember to tell people how you are feeling.

ACCEPTANCE: This doesn't mean that you have accepted (feel OK) that someone has died. It means that you know that they have died and aren't coming back. When you have accepted that someone has died, you can soak up all the love, help and guidance around you.

REMEMBER!
You may not feel these emotions in this order. However, knowing what emotions you are feeling can make it easier to talk about them.

TRY THIS ACTIVITY

Find a backpack and fill it with 5 of your favorite toys. Put on your bag and walk around with it. When it starts to feel heavy, sit down with a grown-up and ask them to read this book with you. As Enid takes an item from her bag, take an item from your bag.

- How does your bag feel when it is full? What about when it is empty?

- Do you think that it is easier or harder to walk with a heavy bag?

- How can you ask a grown-up to help carry some of the heavy items?

- Look for items in your home that remind you of someone who has died.

- Draw a picture of a nice memory that comes into your head when you look at that item.

BEFORE READING

- Read the title of the book. Ask your child if they have ever carried a heavy bag. How did it feel to carry that weight?
- What could you do to help if you saw another child carrying a heavy bag?

WHILE READING

- Enid's grandpa has died. What does the girl at the lemonade stand say that Enid is feeling?
- Why do you think that Enid is feeling angry?
- When did you last feel angry?
- The people that Enid meets all say a rhyme to her. Why do you think they are happy that she shared how she was feeling?
- Fill a bag with heavy items. Ask your child to hold the bag while reading the story. Ask them how it feels to carry the weight by themselves. What might have made it easier for them to carry the bag?

AFTER READING

- How does Enid feel at the end of the book?
- What does the word *grief* mean?
- Does Enid still miss her grandpa?
- Explain that Enid can still miss her grandpa and feel sad/angry/upset some days but sharing these feelings with someone else can make these feelings feel slightly better.
- Is Enid smiling at the end of the book? Why do you think that is?
- Tell your child that it's okay to smile and feel happy even when you miss someone.

AUTHOR
Sarah Surgey

Sarah Surgey has worked within education for the last 17 years in the UK and France. Ten years ago, she began writing as a freelance features writer and later moved into the world of children's books. This is where you will find Sarah at her happiest! By the end of 2023, Sarah will have published 5 children's books in 11 languages. With her concern for children's mental well-being, she most recently worked at a children and families mental health charity and has worked in collaboration with agencies such as UNICEF with her books. Find more at SarahSurgey.com

ILLUSTRATOR
Larisa Ivankovic

Larisa is a freelance illustrator and is very passionate about her work. She has been drawing as long as she can remember and is a fan of many illustration styles. Working in children's publishing keeps her optimistic, sincere, and creative while bringing authors' stories to life. Larisa believes that through colorful and interesting stories we can develop children's imaginations and intelligence.